A First Flight® Level Two Reader

Alice and the Birthday Giant

BY JOHN GREEN

ILLUSTRATED BY MARYANN KOVALSKI

Fitzhenry & Whiteside

FIRST FLIGHT® is a registered trademark of Fitzhenry & Whiteside

Alice and the Birthday Giant
Text copyright © 2000 by John Green
Illustrations copyright © 2000 by Maryann Kovalski

First publication in the United States in 2000.

Fitzhenry & Whiteside acknowledges with thanks the support of the Government of Canada through its Book Publishing Industry Development Program in the publication of this title.

Design by Wycliffe Smith.

10 9 8 7 6 5 4 3 2

Canadian Cataloguing in Publication Data

Green, John F. (John Frederick), 1943-
Alice and the birthday giant

607 101   576804

(A first flight level two reader)
"First flight books".
ISBN 1-55041-538-7 (bound)
ISBN 1-55041-540-9 (pbk.)

I. Kovalski, Maryann. II. Title. III. Series: First flight reader.

PS 8563.R416A8 2000   jC813'.54   C00-930971-3
PZ7.G8234A1 2000

PRIMARY

Dedication

For the two women who made Alice and her giant
come to life, not once but twice...
    Gail Winskill and Maryann Kovalski

John Green

On Saturday morning Alice
was up before anyone else.
She put on her best dress
and combed her hair
very carefully.

Today was her birthday and she was having a party!

"I hope something big happens today," said Alice.

Outside her bedroom door she heard something.

Someone was snoring.
It sounded like an outboard
motor with hiccups.

She pushed the door open.

Sprawled across her bed
was a big, messy
one-eyed giant.

He was sound asleep.
The bed groaned under
his enormous belly.

The bedside lamp rattled
with every snore.

Suddenly, the giant
began to stir.

He stretched his thick,
hairy arms.

He stretched his thick,
hairy legs.

He stretched his huge,
round mouth.

"YaaAAWWWnnn!" he roared.

Then, his one eye saw Alice.

"Who are you?" he growled.

"My name is Alice
and this is *my* bedroom."

"How did I get into
your bedroom?"

"I wished for something
very big to happen
today.

I think you're it,"
Alice said.

The giant's lip stuck out.

"I want to go home!" he bawled.
"That's a good idea," said Alice.
"My father works at the museum
and he'll have you stuffed
in one minute flat."

The giant shivered.

"I have to get ready for my birthday party."

"Yummy!" said the giant, smacking his lips. "I can eat one hundred and eighty-seven hot dogs and fifty-two bowls of ice cream."

Oh dear, thought Alice.

14

Alice took the giant's hand
and led him down the stairs.

She tip-toed past her mother.

"I'll put you in the basement
storage room and figure out
what to do with you later,"
she said.

Soon, it was time
for the party.

Balloons and ribbons hung
all over the kitchen.

The table was covered with
paper plates, hot dogs and
cookies.

All the guests had pointed hats
and horns. There were lots
and lots of presents.

Alice's mother brought in the
strawberry ice cream cake.

Suddenly, there was the sound
of thumping, bumping footsteps
coming up the basement stairs!

Everyone stopped to listen.

Alice knew exactly
what was happening.

"Jumping Jelly Beans!"
she cried.

The basement door crashed open!

There stood the giant.

His belly hung over his belt.

His big round eye stared at everyone.

His bulging nose sniffed the air.

"If it isn't too much trouble," he asked politely, "may I have some hot dogs and ice cream?"

The birthday party went nuts!

Children dove under tables and chairs!

Pickles, hot dogs, ice cream and cake sailed through the room!

And Alice's father ran through the screen door without opening it!

"Look what you've done to my birthday party!" cried Alice.

The giant hung his head. "I want to go home!" wailed the giant.

"When my father comes back he'll have a big net with him for sure."

Suddenly, Alice jumped to her feet.

"Ms. McKracken will help us,"
Alice declared.

"She's the librarian."

Alice sat on the giant's shoulders as they marched through the streets.

People scattered in all directions.

Ms. McKracken took one look
at the giant.

"Where did you come from?"
she asked.
"Someplace with mountains,
I think," grinned the giant.

"I'd better find my book of magic
spells," said Ms. McKracken.

She moved slowly along
the shelves. "Here it is!"

Ms. McKracken turned
the pages of the book.

"Aha! A spell to make a giant
disappear," she exclaimed.

"Wait!" cried the giant.
"I don't want to disappear!"

But it was too late.

"Wham bam billy goat,
Simple Simon in a boat,
Spin a giant's head about,
Make him disappear!"

The library was filled with
a hundred goats floating
in rowboats.

They all bleated loudly.
One of them had a big round eye
right in the middle of his
forehead!

"That didn't work at all,"
muttered Ms. McKracken.
"I'd better try again."

"Purple bats, alley cats,
Thunder, lightning, rain,
Acrobats, floormats,
Bring him back again."

The giant landed in the middle of Ms. McKracken's desk.

"TAKE THAT BOOK
AWAY FROM HER,"
the giant yelled.

With that, the library door
burst open. Alice's father
came in dragging a very
large net behind him.

Ms. McKracken took a deep
breath.

Alice scrunched her eyes shut.

"Forest breeze, mighty trees,
Mountains made of stone.
There's a one-eyed giant here.
Puleeeeze... *send him home!"*

A soft wind rushed
through the room.
It smelled like summer rain.

It lifted papers. It swept through the potted plants and sighed through an open window.

The giant was gone.

"That," said Ms. McKracken, "takes care of that!"

Alice raced home.

She flew upstairs
and opened
her bedroom
door.

She looked under the bed
and inside her closet.

The giant had really disappeared.
"I hope he's gone back to a place
with lots of parties," Alice said
kindly.

She sat down on her bed.
There was a note resting on her
pillow.

It was written in huge crooked
letters.

But Alice didn't see the other
side of the note.

The End